The
Mud Game

SELECTED OTHER BOOKS BY GARY BARWIN

Cruelty to Fabulous Animals (Moonstone Press, 1995)
Scar (Serif of Nottingham, 1994)
Family Relations Are So Complicated (Serif of Nottingham, 1993)
The Iridescent Phlegm of Bagpipers Glorious with Flu (Serif of Nottingham, 1992)
Mollusks of Jealousy (Serif of Nottingham, 1991)
The Stars Are a Pale Pox on the Sky's Dark Chicken (Serif of Nottingham, 1991)
Frogments from the Frag Pool (Proper Tales Press, 1989)
I Parked My Car Behind Loblaws and Knew I Would Never Die (Pink Dog Press, 1989)
What Was Said in Translations (Curvd H&z, 1989)
The Birthday (Gesture Press, 1988)
Ukiah Poems 4 (Underwhich Editions, 1988)
Phases of the Harpsichord Moon (Serif of Nottingham, 1985)

SELECTED OTHER BOOKS BY STUART ROSS

Dusty Hats Vanish (Proper Tales Press, 1994)
The Pig Sleeps (with Mark Laba; Contra Mundo Books, 1993)
Little Black Train (Proper Tales Press, 1993)
In This World (The Berkeley Horse, 1992)
Smothered (Contra Mundo Press, 1990)
Ladies & Gentlemen, Mr. Ron Padgett (Proper Tales Press, 1989)
Paralysis Beach (Pink Dog Press, 1988)
Captain Earmuff's Agenda (The Front Press, 1987)
Skip & Biff Cling to the Radio (Proper Tales Press, 1984)
Tame Me, Mr. Tzara (Curvd H&z, 1982)
Father, the Cowboys Are Ready to Come Down from the Attic (Proper Tales Press, 1982)
He Counted His Fingers, He Counted His Toes (Proper Tales Press, 1978)

The
Mud Game

A NOVEL BY

Gary Barwin and Stuart Ross

THE MERCURY PRESS

The publisher gratefully acknowledges the financial assistance of the Canada Council and the Ontario Arts Council, as well as that of the Government of Ontario through the Ontario Publishing Centre.

Edited by Beverley Daurio
Cover painting by John Ens
Composition and page design by TASK

Printed and bound in Canada by Metropole Litho
Printed on acid-free paper
First Edition
1 2 3 4 5   99 98 97 96 95

Canadian Cataloguing in Publication Data

Barwin, Gary and Ross, Stuart
The mud game
ISBN 1-55128-027-2
I. Title
PS8553.A78M84 1995   C813'.54   C95-932318-x
PR9199.3.B37M84 1995

Represented in Canada by the Literary Press Group
Distributed by General Distribution Services

The Mercury Press
137 Birmingham Street
Stratford, Ontario
Canada   N5A 2T1

The
Mud Game

One

THE MUD GAME

Raymond lay in bed and peered sleepily at the window panes. There must have been a real rain last night, because mud was splashed up from passing cars, and the sun was having trouble getting in. Raymond played the mud game. There, on the bottom left pane, he could make out an image of a Viking. And in the pane above, Raymond saw a horse and its little foals, although some of the foals might have been chickens. The top right didn't hold any image at all, just one narrow streak of muck reaching for the sky, surrounded by all these little muck speckles. Okay, fireworks. Or a comet.

But most miraculous of all was the remaining pane, the bottom right, because this image was actually moving. It was like a windshield wiper on his dad's car, and Raymond just watched in astonishment as it went through its permutations.

Until a dog's face appeared.

"Roadside, is that you?"

You. You. No, wait a second. On second thought. I have been. Rollerskates. Pardon? Yes, far into the garden. A long shoelace like a scar. Like a vein that says How are you? *and then disappears into the lush jungle of your right arm.* How are you? What? You.

A faint orange in the dog's otherwise black eyes made Raymond feel uneasy. He pulled back and the colour seemed to retreat a little farther into the cavelike eyes. He looked across at the other panes. The Viking and the horses had pushed themselves into the caulking of the window frame and were looking nervously up at a sky strewn with the fallout of spent fireworks. The weak light of a comet flickered a bit and then went out.

"I wish you really could be Roadside."

I've. No, you. A grassy plain. Army bodies. It's just that I. Tiny hairs like a paperweight. Impossible? But I. Tarmac. An insect, a rhombus.

The dog's smile was like a broken deck-chair, but Raymond wasn't sure where the voice was coming from. Or even if it was a voice that he was hearing. Then, from the dog's face, pressed close against the glass, a tongue pushed its way out, like one of those fat slugs that Raymond found between the stones in the basement wall. It slid its way across the window, leaving streaks of bubbling saliva where the mud game had been.

Raymond's sheets were covered with rows of identical green cacti, so each morning as he pulled himself out of bed he had to carefully remove the tiny spines from his shoulders and arms and legs. But on this morning, the Morning of the Dog Face Pushed Against the Window, Raymond forgot about the cacti, forgot about breakfast, forgot about school. He reached under his pillow and fished out a small tape recorder. He made a mental note to check later on for groggily narrated dreams, and removed the cassette. From the night-table drawer he took a new tape, slipped it into the recorder, and slowly approached the window.

The dog's nose was now pushed flat against the pane.

"Beg your pardon?" said Raymond, holding the tape recorder up to the glistening nostrils.

Two

GARDENING

"Everything on television is good. Everything in real life is bad." Celia sat down in her chair again and closed her notebook. She had delivered the final pronouncement, the ultimate clincher, the unarguable truth. Might as well basically end the class, close the school, fire the teachers, round up the parents.

Mr. Norton sat back in his own chair, behind his sprawling desk, his cheeks sucked in, his lips slightly puckered. His eyes were bloodshot and he needed a shave. A red vein throbbed on the side of his nose. Without moving his head, he scanned all the faces in his sixth-grade class, looking for one that might offer him some sort of salvation. "Victor?" he said.

The short redhead in the front row remained silent.

"Luciano?"

The boy by the door just twirled his pencil in his fingers.

"Irma...?" he pleaded.

And the bell rang. Mr. Norton heard trumpets. Trumpets at his funeral, flowers drifting down through the clouds to land softly on his fresh grave. The football team sobbing, the history club delivering the benediction.

Celia was out the door before the next day's homework was assigned. She sprinted down the hallway towards her locker, wondering where Raymond had been during her moment of glory. He would certainly have understood the consequences of her statement. He would have agreed that there was no way either of them could ever return to school again. He had always said that if—

A large black dog stood at Celia's locker, guarding the puddle of drool between its front paws.

"Though the hairs of my sleek body look soft, they stick into me like thousands of cactus needles," a voice said from inside the locker.

"Raymond," Celia said, "what are you *doing* in there?"

"Oh, nothing much," Raymond said. "Gardening."

Celia twisted the lock and opened the door. Raymond's gangly frame was squeezed into the space not already filled with Celia's coat, lunchbox, gym shoes, schoolbooks, and a small television set. The inside of the locker door was plastered with photographs clipped from magazines. Mister Ed. Gilligan. Gandhi. George Jetson. A thick layer of dirt covered the locker floor. Several cacti rose from the dirt, and a few more lay on their sides, awaiting installation.

Celia reached up over Raymond and turned on the television. It was the episode of *Three's Company* where Jack believes he is Tolstoy.

"It's perfect," Celia said to no one in particular. "He gives away all his money but he can still afford to dress well and take Chrissie and the other girl, Janet, out to dinner."

The dog, confident of the safety of the now considerable puddle of drool beneath it, stretched out its head and bit into Celia's arm.

"And the thing is," Celia continued, "those people upstairs, the Ropers, never even suspect that he's not still a chef."

Three

THE PHILOSOPHER'S LAWN

"Look, I'll concede that you probably understand Aristotle's *Ethics* or any of Spinoza better than me," Bob the policeman was saying to the philosopher next door, "but I still say a lawn is a lawn, and they don't just disappear like that. Go brown, yes. Get long, sure. Sometimes they even transform—uhh, transmogrify—into weeds or even concrete, but they don't just go missing. It's a new one on me. I wasn't even sure which boxes to check off on the police report. And the funny thing is, that little piece of remaining lawn, just the exact size of the lawn-mower, sure is the most beautiful patch of lawn I've ever seen."

The philosopher looked at him with those almost transparent eyes, clear with a swirly centre like a child's favourite marble. "But it's the sunken dirt, too," he said. "It's got a strange kind of beauty. An otherness. A poetic absence. Like the stillness before song. I once wrote an article—actually it was for *Lawn & Leisure*—where I contrasted the silence of the tiny seeds of grass with the quiet music of the swaying full-grown blades. Really what I was doing was positing a Spinozaic transformation of a universal substantive infinite where the stillness inherent in the nascent lawn is seen as a—granted, more sacred—manifestation of the same unity as the more boisterous mature growth."

Bob raked his hair and let out a low, quiet whistle. "Ellesmere, you've left me in the intellectual dust, and I've got a lot to do today. So let's just say I'll keep my eyes open, and I'll tell Stan, and also Frieda down at the garden store, to keep theirs open, and if I hear anything, I'll get back to you."

The philosopher leaned back in his lawn chair and nodded. "It's that remaining patch of grass, Bob. Makes me wonder. If God, Yahweh, The Big Guy—whatever—decided to make the whole universe disappear, wouldn't there still be a chunk of universe left?"

Bob the policeman shoved his notebook snugly back into his belt and smiled. "A chunk of universe the size and shape of the Lord Himself."

"You know," said Ellesmere, "you might just be ready for a subscription to *Lawn & Leisure*."

Bob's radio was crackling like a breakfast cereal when he returned to his car. "De Groot," he said into the mike.

"Bob," said the dispatcher, "I know you got a lot on your

plate already, but we have reports that a couple of truants just left the park."

"Christ, Diesel," said Bob, "I'm about to go on lunch. Let Mr. Asshole take care of his own." Mr. Asshole was Mr. Ashwell, the school principal. Little Bob De Groot had been one of his prize victims about twenty years earlier, and it caused Officer Bob a lot of pain to do the old man's bidding.

The radio hissed and popped. "Yeah, Bob, but politics, y'know. Maybe you could just take a quick look, hustle the punks back to school, slap their wrists, make the little old ladies happy, right?"

"Okay, okay," said the weary officer. "Just do this for me: tell Stan to keep his eyes peeled for a pickup full of sod, or any kind of mysterious cache of grass—lawn grass. I'll mention it to Frieda Viking-Norton, too. My neighbour, Ellesmere Dunkirk, woke up to find his lawn AWOL. Just dirt and worms left, Diesel. Dirt and worms."

Four

THE LAWN CIRCLE

Leaves tumbled across the empty soccer field behind the plaza. Raymond and Celia sat on a log under a huge, drooping tree. Between them was the black dog, its wrinkled eyelids crusted with dried mucus.

"Television, Raymond," Celia said. "I'm talking about television and reality. I beat the system. I made the establishment crumble."

Raymond drew a deep breath, fingering the tape recorder hidden under his red windbreaker. "I was playing the mud game. You know how it goes. You know the mud game."

"Mr. Norton freaked. He just looked around the room, waiting to be saved. He didn't know what to say."

"The cacti in your locker, Celia. Don't you understand?"

Celia pounded a small, soft fist against the log. "C'mon, Raymond! You think you know everything! Can't *I* maybe have a bit of the glory?!"

The dog began to bark, snapping its yellow teeth at a

circling fly. In its eyes, an orange glow began to appear. Sticks were being rubbed together, and sparks were leaping.

This. Where? Oh 10-10-10. Can't really. The blue and. Shh. No, please, who? I am Jack Tripper and I. Endless ore. If gymnastics, can't. A hydrogen molecule. Tufts.

"Shit, Raymond, what *is* that?"

"That's what I was trying to tell you, Ceely. Right during the mud game." Raymond fumbled with the tape recorder, pushing the red record button as he held the microphone to the dog's face. "Sounds like the dog's picking up some kind of TV signal. It's just like in the mud game, Ceely. Something's trying to tell me something. Something we don't understand. Look, whatever this is, this isn't Roadside. I don't know what happened to Roadside or where she is, but this isn't my dog. It's not even real."

"Roadside?" said Celia. "Roadside's dead."

On the. This is. Gnash. Yeah, right. Sorry, what? Green seventh. The wren that fled. Iron beside me. West cut. No. A worm that.

Raymond hit the rewind button on the tape recorder and then pressed play.

Nothing.

"See, Celia? This happened the other times, too. Whatever that voice is, it doesn't record. And back at school, when it bit you, you didn't even feel it, right?"

"What do you mean I didn't feel it? Look." Celia rolled up her shirtsleeve, revealing the red ring of a dog bite on her upper arm. Where each tooth had sunk into her, a tiny blade of grass had begun to grow.

Five

DOG RING

Ellesmere Dunkirk tilted his head back and drained the bottle of Ethic Lager.

"Yes, indeed," he said, pushing his squat feet into the sandals beside the deck-chair. He stepped down from the square of lawn raised like a dais in the centre of his yard of mud, and proceeded towards the sliding doors at the back of his house. He slid open the screen door and was about to open the glass door when he thought better of it and turned to look around.

A ring of small white dogs had formed about the square of sod. They seemed to be softly barking, but it was a kind of arf the philosopher didn't recognize. They were circling slowly, each with the tail of the dog before it in its mouth.

Ellesmere rubbed his eyes and head and then sighed. He went inside the house and picked up the phone. He placed the receiver back in its cradle after dialing a single number.

The sun was throwing light the colour of spilled beer

through the rustling kitchen curtain. Ellesmere Dunkirk sat down at the kitchen table with a pencil and opened a notebook. *Ring of Dogs,* he wrote at the top of the first page. He paused. Then he scratched it out and wrote *Circle of Puppies* below it. He drew a small square below that and passed out.

Six

LUNCH BREAK

"Where you going, Seth? Can I join you?" Caroline Carson looked up from her take-out Caesar salad. She had had her eye on Seth Norton for a long time now, ever since news of his marriage break-up had gotten around.

But Seth didn't respond. In fact, he crossed the staff lounge like a sleepwalker, without acknowledging even Mr. Ashwell, the school principal. Seth draped his light jacket over his shoulders and headed for the door. Everyone watched. Everyone was quiet.

Caroline was right behind Seth as he left the school through the side doors and shuffled across the parking lot, out onto the sidewalk. She watched him continue down the street, and she followed on the other side. He was heading towards a small row of shops.

In front of one of the windows, Seth Norton paused and pushed his hands deep into his trouser pockets. Caroline peered through the lunch-hour traffic and saw that he had planted himself before the window of Ziptron Television, where about a dozen TV sets were all tuned to a commercial for pool supplies. After a few minutes, Seth tilted his head back and began to wail. He clawed at the window as the television images switched in unison to two women facing each other in a restaurant, wine glasses in hand.

Caroline Carson made her way across the street, weaving between the slow-moving cars, until she reached her colleague. "Seth," she said quietly, placing her hands on his shoulders. "Seth, it's going to be okay."

Seth swung around and collapsed into her arms, sobbing and snuffling. "C-C-Caroline," he murmured. "She knows, she knows, Celia knows..." His body shook and heaved against hers.

She stroked his hair and tried to steady him by holding him still closer. "Seth...Seth..." she said, soothingly. "Let's talk about this. Let's—"

And then he pulled himself free, roughly pushing Caroline aside. With all his energy, Seth Norton threw himself against the window of the television shop. For a moment he appeared glued to the glass, completely motionless. Then it all began to cave in, and he fell forward into the stack of TVs, the women of the afternoon soaps collapsing onto him.

Seven

SHARP HAIRS

Raymond held Celia's arm in his hands and sniffed the tiny blades of grass. "You glue these on?"

"And from each tooth did sprout a miniature life."

"Celia, you're giving me the creeps. You and this dog both." Raymond tugged gently at one of the growths and snapped it off. "Oh, yeah, see, they come right off!"

Of the steam shovel. Eyes towards. Factual! Factual! With this tiny crystal. Pantomime. Don't you speaking. Crusty towards. $34.95. A terrible velocity.

"Raymond!" sneered Celia, pulling her arm away. "Would you make that weird dog shut up!"

This tune. Four in the. Spinoza bird. Not home right now, may I? And come spring.

Celia reached over and held the dog's mouth shut, but the voice continued. "We've got to do something about this, Raymond."

"About what?" said a voice from behind them.

Celia, Raymond, and the dog jumped. "Officer De Groot!" said Celia.

Raymond leapt to his feet. "Run, Roadside!" he yelled. Celia looked at him sharply as he slapped a hand over his mouth. The dog stood its ground, its wet eyes peering silently into the face of the patrolman.

Bob sank slowly to his knees and stared back at the dog. "Run? Well, Roadside, why would you want to run? Been digging up anyone's lawns lately?" He laughed and looked from Raymond to Celia. "Maybe you kids can help me solve a little mystery. There's an absence at the school. Two students are missing, and the pockets of space there are just about your size."

Celia crossed her arms slowly, hiding the ring of lawn that poked up through the tooth impressions on her arm.

De Groot pulled himself to his feet. The dog's jaws opened, then closed around his leg. A broad smile came over the man's face.

I've got a. Low lying shrubs. Y'know how it. A border guard. The skipper and. Tennis. Oblong. Tennis.

For the brief moment that the dog's teeth were clamped around the policeman's leg there was no sound other than the dog's strange voice. Then it released its jaws and Bob De Groot began to speak.

"The rising grasses are the absence of lawn. Their sharp hairs are the hairs of dogs, the needles on the cacti's arms," De Groot said. "I have lain on the lawn as if on a bed of glass, have seen the hundred eyes of the television shatter."

"Y'know what this reminds me of?" Celia said. "It reminds me of the episode of *Gunsmoke* where the sheriff gets kicked in the head by a horse."

In Raymond's head, a little piece fell into place. "What did he sing?" Raymond asked.

"'How Much Is That Doggie in the Window?'" Celia replied.

Eight

SOFT HAIRS

In the public pool at the park, everything was calm, everything was still. It was like a giant TV set showing a picture of the sky. And Caroline Carson was the only one there. She stripped down and leapt off the diving board. The still, blue surface shattered the way a store window shatters when a teacher goes through it. The way twelve identical plots shatter when a teacher knocks over the entire stack of TVs at Ziptron Television.

But beneath the surface, it was calm again. Regular programming had resumed and Caroline swam along the pool's grassy floor. The cool waters soothed her and the soft blades caressed her skin. Caroline forgot the details of the world above her—they became nothing more than a play of light on the pool's screen.

Life had once been so simple, but that was before she joined the Philosophers' Club. She had thought it was important for a teacher to keep learning, and Ellesmere Dunkirk's club had seemed like such a good idea. Besides, Seth Norton had already joined.

The philosopher would often read to the club, articles that he was writing for *Lawn & Leisure*. Seth in particular was interested in Dunkirk's notion of the lawn chair as the secularization of a pantheistic conception of leisure, while she felt sympathetic towards—if not wholly convinced by—his belief in the doghouse as the *locus in quo* for a drama of pure forms.

They would argue sometimes till early morning, drinking prodigious quantities of Ellesmere's beloved Ethic Lager.

The club met every second Thursday, and Seth would pull up at the door to Caroline's apartment building in his little sports car with the top down. They had discussed Leibnitz, Hume, Aquinas, and Hobbes at the first meeting she attended, but she had spoken to Seth of Descartes during the car ride home.

Once, before his divorce, Caroline had woken to find herself in Seth Norton's arms. He was asleep, and so she quietly slipped out of the car.

But looking at it now, it wasn't so simple: one couldn't just spend the night refuting the *Discourse on Method* on the basis of the current valorization of the pest as a mechanism of unconscious seed control and then forget everything.

There were other people involved. What about Seth's ex-wife, Frieda? What about one's daughter? Yes, one's daughter. Celia. Is that what Seth meant when he said she *knew*? Is that what he meant just before he threw himself through the window? Shit. No one was supposed to know, let alone her own daughter.

Caroline swam the length of the pool in one breath, flipped around and then swam towards a squat shape in the pool's centre. She swam so that the grass on the pool's floor brushed against her body. She entered the submerged dog-house. Aroused.

Nine

HEADS 'N' CRACKERS

Raymond walked into Viking Cactus & Flower with a question. Frieda Viking-Norton was standing behind the counter.

"What can I do for you today, Raymond?" she asked, chopping the end off a small cactus that lay in front of her.

Raymond watched her cut the cactus into small slices, then place them onto some crackers set out on a plate.

"I know a good recipe for jam," Raymond finally said. "And it works with just about every kind of cactus."

"I had some of your jam over at Mr. Ashwell's place," Frieda replied. "It was really very good."

"Uh, thanks," said Raymond. He could not imagine where Asshole had got hold of his jam— unless it had been when he and Celia had spread it over the windshield of the principal's car. The windshield had been a sticky green mess, little needles poking up everywhere like blades of grass. Bob De Groot had looked at it and laughed, then yelled at Raymond in front of the whole school.

"Mrs. Viking..." he began, cautiously. "You were there when it happened, and there's something I have to know."

Frieda popped a cactus cracker into her mouth, sucking hard to soften the little spines. "When what happened, Raymond?"

"You know," he continued. "Roadside. They never told me what happened to her, just that it happened out front here, and they said you fainted."

Frieda tossed another cracker into her mouth. "Raymond," she said through cactus meat and cracker fragments, "I promised your folks I'd never tell. They want to save you a lot of pain."

"This morning I was gardening in Celia's locker again. You know—Celia Carson. The soil was dry and seemed at first unworkable. But desert soil doesn't need much, Mrs. Viking, and I worked patiently until the locker floor was able to open its arms to my little cacti."

A bell rang and a man in a suit walked into the store and began browsing among the tulips.

Raymond lowered his voice and continued. "There was a dog outside the locker, and she looked a lot like old Roadside. I tried to ignore her and continue gardening. You know how clearly you can think when you're out working the cacti. So I was trying to think and clear up everything in my mind, but all I could hear was this dog panting in the hallway outside the locker. And everyone tells me Roadside's gone, but the other morning there's this dog outside my window, and I know it can't be Roadside, but—"

"Raymond," Frieda interrupted. "Let me tell you something. A few minutes ago I received a call. It was the hospital. Seth—my ex-husband—leapt through a store window into a stack of television sets. They think he'll live, but he may never teach again. I said, 'You think I care? You think I care what happens to that bastard?' and I hung up the phone. But of course I care, Raymond. And maybe some morning I'll be lying in bed, playing the mud game, you know? And there will be Seth, his nose pressed against the glass. As if to say, 'Take me back, take me back, my little Viking.' That's what he used to call me. His little Viking." Frieda was carefully stacking the remaining cactus crackers in a tin box. "Raymond, Roadside leapt through a window, too. Right there, across the road where Bellini Real Estate used to be. Who knows what Roadside saw in that window? But I was out talking to your dad, who'd let Roadside off the lead. We both watched as the window came down on her, severing her neck."

Raymond began to feel weak. He leaned against the counter for support.

"Roadside's body just leapt back to its feet, headless, and galloped in circles until it disappeared around the corner. No one wanted to follow and see what happened. The head—Roadside's head— just lay there where it had landed. Right in Alberto Bellini's lap."

The man in the suit approached the counter with several orange tulips. "Soccer season," he said, then smiled. "How much?"

Raymond took a few tentative steps from the counter and made for the door.

He had to talk to someone.

He had to talk to Celia.

He had to talk to the dog.

Ten

BROKEN BOTTLE

"Turn left here," Celia said, "right before the soccer field."

Bob De Groot turned the steering wheel of his police car sharply, his empty eyes glazed and bloodshot. "The blades of the cactus," he said, his words lost beneath the unrelenting bark of the siren.

"Now make a left and then a quick right," Celia said.

The police car lurched around the corner as Bob spun the wheel again. The car bounced up over the curb, skidded through a bed of tulips and across a lawn, finally breaking through a fence and crashing into the dais of grass in the centre of Ellesmere Dunkirk's yard. Throughout all of this, the dog in the back seat had remained perfectly silent, perfectly still. It was only when the most beautiful patch of lawn that Bob had ever seen sailed through the air and smashed against the windshield that the dog began to howl with the siren.

"The hairs of my arm are the hairs of lawn," Bob said.

Celia climbed out of the car and looked around. Small puppies were everywhere, running in circles. She began walking towards Ellesmere's door, but then stopped and lay down on the bare soil. The puppies crowded over her, nipping her shoulders, her legs, her arms. "Everything on television is good," Celia said. "Everything in real life is bad."

The dog jumped out the police car window and waited for Bob. Together they walked through Ellesmere Dunkirk's open sliding doors. Beer bottles lay all around the paper-strewn room. A television was on, but the sound had been turned down. On the screen, a reporter stood in front of Ziptron Television's shattered window, pointing at twelve broken TV sets.

Bob walked into the kitchen. Ellesmere Dunkirk was slumped back in a chair at the table. A broken bottle of Ethic lay in a pool of foam just below his dangling hand. On the table, a notebook lay open. Bob looked at the square drawn in the centre of the notebook page. He lifted a pencil from the table and made a large checkmark in the middle of the square.

Then Bob tore the page from the notebook and placed it in Ellesmere's breast pocket. He walked to the window, peering out at his own house next door. Two neat parallel trails lay diagonally across his lawn, and his tulips were a disgrace. "I know which boxes to check, Chief. I know which boxes to check."

The dog watched as Bob De Groot undid his belt and stepped out of his blue trousers. He loosened his tie and peeled back his shirt. "Hold this," said Bob, extending his gun to the inert philosopher.

Celia was still prone on the naked ground, submerged in her puppy-induced euphoria. She was unaware as the underwear-clad Bob stepped over her, making for the street. The thin blades of grass danced on her arm, and the tiny puppy-nips throbbed in her shoulders and legs.

A few minutes later, a few blocks away, Patrolman Bob walked along the narrow path through the park. He came to a stop at the end of a swimming pool. The sheet of still water reflected pure blue on Bob's face, and, having never swum a stroke in his life, Bob plunged into the water and glided across the silky, undulating pool floor towards a shimmering dog-house.

On the diving board above the deep end, the black dog lay down to sleep.

Left her when. A dozen TVs. Don't. Rachmaninov never. Exciting new. Towards. Shards. And have you met. Critical condition.

Eleven

GERMS

"Roadside, I can see you leaping from the shattered window, running around in circles in the street, and everyone's scream- ing, until you disappear around a corner and run headless down an alleyway. You're bumping into garbage cans and tripping over bundles of newspapers, Roadside, and you don't know where your head is, you don't understand what's hap- pened to you. I told Dad to keep you on the leash, not to let you off, because I knew you liked to chase cars and I didn't want you getting run over. And then Grandpa would have to pick you up by your hind legs like a chicken and put you in a garbage bag and leave you at the front of the lawn so they could pick you up like they did with the Rolands' dog.

"Roadside, it seems so unreal when I come home and you're not there, jumping on me, nearly knocking me over. I could scratch your hair and your ears and take off your collar when it gets too hot, because I don't like it when you choke. Roadside, there are things that are so hard for me. Like in math—I get confused by all those numbers, and now Mrs. Cobb says we have to do algebra—and there's no way I'll be able to figure that stuff out.

"When you were running away, Roadside, did you know what you were doing, because if your brain is in your head, how can your body think, but what use is a brain in a head if there's no body attached? But maybe your thinking went into your body, Roadside.

"Come on, lie here on my feet and let me tell you things. In history they want us all to write down ten reasons why we shouldn't have wars and then ten reasons why people start them anyway. And there's explosions and screaming and when the smoke clears away, you can see soldiers lying halfway out of the trenches. Some of your favourite actors, too. Army bodies. But on a black-and-white television the blood's grey, it's not red like in real life.

"You were smarter than to go near cactus plants, because you knew that the spines could stick you, Roadside. And you knew that cacti grow in deserts, but if there's enough of them, it's not a desert any more. It's a forest. Everyone said you were nice, but sometimes you just got carried away. Like that time Celia came over and you bit her arm and Victor said they'd probably shoot you, but Celia didn't cry and she didn't get sick. Sometimes Dad jokes and says I'll marry Celia and he punches me in the arm, but I told him Celia's smarter than me, and she knows about television, so I can't marry her.

"Lick the window clean, Roadside. It doesn't matter if dogs get their tongues dirty, because Mom says you lick yourself in dirty places anyway but you don't die from the germs. I won't let you off the leash, Roadside—just lick the window."

Twelve

A BED OF GLASS

Seth Norton pressed the button to call the nurse. About five minutes later, a short dark-haired woman entered his private room.

"Nurse, could you turn the channel for me, please," he asked weakly. "I can't stand to keep watching myself jump through the window like that. You'd think it was the assassination of a president or something."

Nurse Button reached up and turned the dial on the television above the bed. "Is this okay?" she said.

"Yes, thanks," Seth replied. Though *Three's Company* was not his favourite show, it was certainly better than watching himself dive through the window of Ziptron Television. And those reporters—what did they know? No, it was certainly better to be watching Jack and Chrissie swimming in the public pool. Jack had stripped down to his boxer shorts and jumped into the water after Chrissie, who was swimming nude. Seth knew this wasn't real. He'd seen Jack's—uh, John

Ritter's—new series and also his movies. He'd seen Suzanne Sommers lecture once about alcoholism down at Ethic Brewery, and he'd seen her replacement after she left the show, though he couldn't remember her name. While John Ritter—Jack—swam after Chrissie, a large black animal—he couldn't quite make out what it was—waited on the deck beside the pool. The animal stood up. God, it had no head. It just stood there, as if it were barking. As if it were calling out. Then from somewhere inside the television, from somewhere behind the picture of the dog, something flew out at the screen and smashed against it. Glass went everywhere. There were twelve screens now and Seth Norton saw Caroline, saw Mr. Ashwell, saw goddamned Frieda all jump through the screen. He saw half his fucking sixth-grade class come flying through.

He couldn't breathe.

The nurse came in and turned the channel. A president folded to the sidewalk.

Thirteen

ELEVEN YEARS OLD

Celia pulled herself to her feet. As she looked down and saw that she was up to her ankles in mud, she became aware of a steady trickle of rain. There were no puppies, and no little puppy footprints. She looked at her arms and they were white and smooth. Where were the red circle of teeth and the slender blades of grass that had protruded from it?

Celia distinctly remembered standing in front of her school locker that morning—just after her school-closing pronouncement—and watching the big black dog sink its teeth into her bare arm. Where had that dog come from, anyway? Raymond had brought it. Raymond, who was planting cacti on the soil-covered floor of her locker. Peat moss would have been better. She should have told him.

A few metres away, an empty police car, doors wide open, was wheel-deep in the softening earth. The front of the car was buried in a raised mound, and the windshield was a chaotic web. Clods of grass were scattered about the vehicle and its radio emitted a steady hymn of static.

Celia was eleven years old and she was standing drenched on a neighbourhood lawn that had been stripped of grass. She was eleven years old and she had brought down her teacher and her school. What was it she had said? She had said, "TV good. Life bad." Or something to that effect. What had she been talking about, she wondered.

The door of the house was open and rain was streaming onto the yellow kitchen floor. Celia could make out the dark shape of a man in a chair. It was Ellesmere Dunkirk. She'd been at this house before; she recognized it even without its perfectly groomed lawn. Celia's mother came here a couple of times a month for the Philosophers' Club. She was always talking about Dunkirk and his writings, his column in *Lawn & Leisure*, his theories on Spinoza and seedlings and man's inherent power.

Celia thought Spinoza was a stupid name. He sounded like a cartoon spider. "No, he was a Dutch Jew," Caroline Carson had explained. "He was ostracized and virtually excommunicated by both his religion and his country." "Still sounds like a Walt Disney character to me," Celia had retorted.

A worm emerged from the wet soil and surveyed the lawn like a periscope, just as Celia herself had done. Police car: check. Mound of dirt: check. Pile of blue clothing: check. Drenched girl: check. Open screen door: check. Girl moving towards screen door: check. Girl peering into kitchen from patio: check.

Ellesmere Dunkirk sat by his kitchen table, one hand clutching a gun in his lap, the other reaching towards the floor where a shattered bottle lay. Celia entered, tracking mud across the linoleum, and she stood over the philosopher. Had he killed himself?

She saw no blood.

There was, however, a piece of paper sticking out of his breast pocket. Gingerly, Celia removed it, and as she did, she became aware of the blinking red from the police car. The whole kitchen lit up every few seconds. Celia read the note.

Ring of Dogs. This was crossed out.

Circle of Puppies, printed carefully underneath.

And below this, a square with a checkmark in it.

None of it connected, thought Celia. She walked over to the fridge and took out a carton of milk. She sat down across from Dunkirk and drank. "What's your point?" she asked him.

And as she waited for his motionless jaw to answer, Celia

remembered the big black dog again. Raymond's dog. Road-side. It had spoken. Well, it seemed to have spoken, but, like Ellesmere Dunkirk, its mouth hadn't moved.

She placed the empty milk carton in the philosopher's lap and headed for home.

The rain was falling harder now and Celia had to tug her feet out of the mud with every step. "Ugh," she said.

Fourteen

LOST LAWN

Forty-eight hours later, the rains still hadn't abated. And down at the police station, reported sightings of the missing lawn had been arriving in a steady trickle.

"Somehow things just don't seem right with my neighbour's lawn. It seems too...thick."

"There was this whole family down by the mall. They were all carrying identical suitcases and I saw a trail of grass behind them."

"I saw a bunch of men carrying pieces of sod. They were filing into the elevator of Ethic Brewery."

"This morning when I went to get dressed, I found grass in my sock drawer, grass in my suit jacket."

"When I looked in the window, there was grass on the floors of that school they just closed down."

A teller from the Savemore 'N' Loan Bank phoned in on the emergency line, claiming that two men were trying to deposit sections of lawn into a savings account.

Schools closing.

Stolen lawns.

Officer De Groot's car abandoned on his neighbour's lawn.

Teachers jumping through windows.

The public pool shut down.

Raymond, the school trustee's son, missing.

Stan Bluebody didn't have any idea where to begin his investigation. And on top of everything else, the phone lines were down, the streets flooded. His bowling night had been cancelled.

Christ, he thought, and helped himself to another slice of cactus.

Fifteen

IN THE CENTRE OF LAWN

In the park, the steady drumming of rain on the doghouse roof was relentless. It was driving Bob crazy.

"Listen, Caroline," he said, "we've surfaced. I just have to go out and stretch my legs a bit."

Caroline, curled up in the far corner of the doghouse, stirred in her sleep. Bob pushed back the flap of carpet covering the doghouse door and crawled through the small opening. The lawn outside gave way beneath his step, then rose again like the rolling waves of a waterbed. Bob put his hand out, steadied himself against the doghouse.

In the dim light, everything around him was grey. Even the red doors of the change rooms were grey.

The entire park was covered in several feet of water. He could just make out the top of the children's water fountain, trickling feebly into the wind. A tree had fallen onto the set of swings by the park's entrance. The street beyond was empty and the houses along it were dark.

"The lawn has risen to meet the falling waters," Bob said, his soft voice drifting across the flooded park. "We are alone in our doghouse in the centre of the lawn, in the centre of the flood," he continued. "The circle of dogs is now complete, the needles of the cactus broken."

Behind him, the flap of carpet was pulled aside, and Caroline's pale head emerged. "Got a cigarette, Bob?" she said.

Sixteen

VISITING HOURS

Frieda tugged open the lid of the tin of crackers on her lap. Empty. She peered out the bus window and watched the trees and telephone poles whip by. Cows, barns, and mailboxes were a blur. The clouds were breaking now, and the fading sun spread an orange glow across the fields.

Celia's head on her shoulder was a comfort. Frieda reached across with her left hand and stroked the girl's hair. "We're almost there, Ceely," she said. "Almost there."

Just visible beyond the next rise were the tips of skyscrapers poking into a blanket of rolling smog.

"Is it really true what you told Raymond? About that Bellini guy, I mean?" asked Celia.

"There's only one way to find out." Frieda's back was in knots, but she didn't know whether it was because of the rains, or the long bus journey in this impossible seat.

They had already been way behind schedule when the bus pulled out of the terminal, carting its passengers through the flooded streets. And then the flat tire had conspired to slow them down even more. The driver had climbed into the bus again after three-quarters of an hour in the rain, holding up a grease-coated hand. "We're on our way, folks. Just a cactus spine. I've patched the sucker up and we'll have no further trouble."

Celia rubbed her eyes and leaned across Frieda, looking out over the rapidly changing fields. "I had a dream," she explained. "We were all in school and Mr. Ashwell came on over the PA system and told everyone to assemble right away in the cafeteria. So there we were in the cafeteria—I mean, we didn't even have to walk there: we were just there, like it happens in a dream, you know?—and Asshole—that's what we call him—Asshole was standing at the front, holding up a big piece of glass covered in a sort of green jelly. He said, into the microphone, 'I'll get the culprit.' Then he ran his thumb through the jelly and poked it into his mouth. Every-body laughed. Then Raymond stood up on one of the tables and said, 'Look at the shape in the window! Look at the shape you made in the jelly! It's Roadside!'"

Frieda seemed not to be listening. "When we find Mr. Bellini, Celia, we have to be very, very careful. If he doesn't remember us, don't be scared. I've packed another tin of cactus crackers and first we'll present that as a gift from everybody in town. Then you can ask him anything you want, but if he starts getting upset, you've got to slow down."

Celia held up her schoolbag. "I wrote down all my questions. They start off gradually, then they get to the good stuff."

Frieda's mind wandered back to Seth. It was frightening to think that she'd actually spent so many of her years with a man who would leap through a window into a bank of television sets. "What was it you said to Mr. Norton again, Celia?" she asked.

"I asked him why he killed Roadside," the girl replied.

Then the whole bus shuddered as the driver switched into a lower gear. They were entering the city, and the sounds of the traffic, the sidewalks, and the music blaring from the shops filled the vehicle.

Frieda Viking-Norton looked at her watch. "We'll make it just before visiting hours end, I think."

Seventeen

LIGHTS OUT

Stan Bluebody climbed out of his police car, walked up the lawn to George Ashwell's house, and rang the doorbell. The policeman looked down at the smug rows of orange tulips on either side of the porch. After a few moments, Ashwell's wife, Chrissie, answered the door. A small child held on to one of her legs.

"Hello there, Mrs. Ashwell," Stan said, lifting his hat. "And hello there, Janet," he said to the child, smiling. "Aren't you a big girl now."

"Say hello to Officer Bluebody," Chrissie Ashwell said. The child hid behind her mother's legs. "You're probably looking for George, right?"

Stan nodded.

"I'm afraid George was kicked in the head by a horse. George jumped through a window. George was singing 'Let

It Be' and was bitten by a dog. George is mowing the lawn," she said.

Seth Norton rolled over in his hospital bed. Shards of sticky green glass slid off the bed and fell to the floor. The large dog in the chair beside his bed turned towards him.

Listen, it said. *We've gotta ride this one out.*

The sound on the black-and-white television above the bed was turned down. A reporter pointed to a flooded downtown intersection. The traffic lights were out and cars waded cautiously around a policeman who was desperately trying to sort out the chaos.

Eighteen

EGO TE ABSOLVO

It had been quite a surprise, waking up with a carton of milk and a gun in his lap, but Ellesmere Dunkirk had had surprises before. Like not being drafted to the major leagues. Like finding out he wasn't adopted. Like catching his foot in the lawn-mower.

Milk had dribbled out of the carton onto Ellesmere's pants. It had made him think of something. He had looked down. A foot of water covered the kitchen floor, and a beer bottle was bobbing up and down near his left leg. He had stroked his chin ponderously and murmured, "That's a hell of a lot of stubble for an afternoon nap."

Having considered the matter while drying off in his second-floor study, Ellesmere flipped on his television set. The Philosophers' Club would be meeting that night, and he liked to be up-to-date, liked to blend the day's world events into the grand arena of Spinoza, Hume, and Wittgenstein.

On the screen a reporter was pointing to a policeman talking to a woman and child on a suburban porch. In the foreground, in the centre of a lawn, a man lay bandaged in a bed, watching television. A large black dog sat in a chair beside the man's bed. The man was watching a television set—a small black-and-white—and on the screen a reporter was pointing at a cop directing traffic in a flooded, chaotic intersection.

Ellesmere looked back over his shoulder. Behind him, a puppy was perched on his filing cabinet, its fur matted and filthy. The philosopher hurled a TV guide at the dog, who leapt clear just in time. "How'd you get in here?" demanded Ellesmere.

The dog barked a small bark and bounded from the room and down the stairs.

When Ellesmere Dunkirk turned his attention back to the television screen, the news was already over, and some stupid comedy show was on. He surveyed the characters and decided that he hated all of them and could never really bring himself to care about their fates.

Ellesmere went downstairs and hefted the gun that he had placed on the kitchen table. Then he opened the fridge and placed the gun in an open jar. He watched as the weapon sank through the thick green jelly.

Not completely satisfied, Ellesmere rummaged through the flooded cupboard under his sink until he found a length of strong chain. He wound this around the refrigerator and heaved the elephantine appliance over on its side. Was it his imagination, or did a dozen yapping puppies help him drag it out the door and onto the naked lawn, where the Cold-O-Rama sank into the mud, emitting a thick bubble every now and then.

Nineteen

HER MASTER'S VOICE

With a steady paw, she pushed the button on the tape recorder. *Roadside, I can see you leaping from a shattered window...*

Twenty

A PROPERTY THING

Frieda Viking-Norton and Celia Carson walked tentatively up the path to the clubhouse. The dirty brown stubble of lawn around them was relieved only by untidy beds of orange flowers. The sign on the door read Anubis Realty Bloodhounds. Then below: Winners, National Soccer Championship, 1956.

Frieda rang the doorbell. Immediately the door swung open.

"Visiting hours have begun," said a squat grey-haired man in a white suit, waving them in. They were led down a narrow hallway and into a little room at the back of the clubhouse. The man sat them down at a small table surrounded by more orange flowers.

"Greetings," he said. "I'm Alberto Bellini. You must be Celia. And you, Frieda Viking-Norton."

"Yes," Celia said nervously. "We brought you this—from everyone." She handed him the silver tin of crackers.

"It's been a long time. We didn't think you would know who we were," Frieda said.

"I don't," he answered. "I have friends down at the bus terminal."

"I see," Frieda replied softly. "We'd like to ask you a few questions, Mr. Bellini."

"We were the National Soccer Champions in 1956," the man snapped.

"I saw that on the door," said Frieda. "We've come here to ask about the dog."

The man's face paled. "What did you say your name was?" he asked.

"Look, Mr. Bellini—Alberto—you were there when it happened. Celia has a few questions to ask you. Seth's in the hospital. He jumped through the window of Ziptron Television. Ray Firth's son Raymond is missing. Please, will you do this for me?" Frieda put her hand on Bellini's shoulder.

"Nineteen-fifty-six," he said, after a long pause.

Celia took a small notepad from her schoolbag and flipped it open. She read the first question. "Mr. Bellini, what exactly were you doing at the moment that Roadside leapt through your window?"

Bellini fiddled with his tie. "I was, uh, making a phone call. You know, a property thing. A property for sale."

"Mr. Bellini, at what moment did you become aware of the canine decapitation?"

Bellini lifted a trophy off his desk. "Have I shown you the trophy?"

Celia just stared into the pages of her notebook. She couldn't face the white-suited man. "Maybe it was when Roadside's head landed in your lap?"

"I heard Raymond scream," said Bellini. "We were practising—I was in goal—and I heard him scream."

"You mean Mr. Firth?" interjected Frieda.

"The kid," said Bellini. "Norton held the dog around its middle and then kept ramming its head against my window. I sell real estate, you know."

Celia cleared her throat. "Mr. Bellini, is a dog a TV, or what?"

"I just call it a lawn," said Alberto Bellini. "I stick a sign in it and the sign says For Sale. It's your own thing, right? A lawn. It's yours. No one else can have it."

Celia looked up from her pages.

"I can sell it for you, though. Do you want to get rid of it?" Bellini reached out and took one of Frieda's hands. "Look," he said, dragging one of his fingernails under the tip of one of her own. "Dirt. Soil. You been gardening?" He stared right into her eyes. "Or you been licking yourself in dirty places?"

"What the hell you mean by that?" Seth Norton shouted at the nurse. He swung his legs out of the hospital bed and tried to stand on the lawn, but it gave way under his weight, then rose again in slow waves. "I certainly have not been licking myself," he yelled. He reached over and turned the sound down. Nurse Button pointed at him. "I have just one more question for you," she said, and then shattered. The head fell into Ellesmere's milky lap. He put his squat foot to the police car's grassy floor. The car shuddered as it passed into high gear and skidded across the lawn, into an alleyway between two houses. God, I have no head, Bob's body thought and then screamed. Chrissie, come quick, the Ropers know I am no chef. Tulips waded through the flooded streets, or maybe chickens. Caroline let out a low whistle.

(Raymond rubbed two sticks together. A spark. "Good Roadside," he said. "Good girl.")

1957.